Dear Parent:
Your child's love of reading starts here!

Every child learns to read in a different way and at his or her own speed. Some go back and forth between reading levels and read favorite books again and again. Others read through each level in order. You can help your young reader improve and become more confident by encouraging his or her own interests and abilities. From books your child reads with you to the first books he or she reads alone, there are I Can Read Books for every stage of reading:

SHARED READING
Basic language, word repetition, and whimsical illustrations, ideal for sharing with your emergent reader

BEGINNING READING
Short sentences, familiar words, and simple concepts for children eager to read on their own

READING WITH HELP
Engaging stories, longer sentences, and language play for developing readers

READING ALONE
Complex plots, challenging vocabulary, and high-interest topics for the independent reader

ADVANCED READING
Short paragraphs, chapters, and exciting themes for the perfect bridge to chapter books

I Can Read Books have introduced children to the joy since 1957. Featuring award-winning authors and illustrat fabulous cast of beloved characters, I Can Read Books se standard for beginning readers.

A lifetime of discovery begins with the magical words "I Can Read!"

Visit www.icanread.com for information
on enriching your child's reading experience.

I Can Read!

READING 2 WITH HELP

DREAMWORKS

HOW TO TRAIN YOUR

DRAGON

Hiccup the Hero

I Can Read Book® is a trademark of HarperCollins Publishers.

How to Train Your Dragon: Hiccup the Hero
How to Train Your Dragon™ & © 2010 DreamWorks Animation L.L.C. All rights reserved.
www.icanread.com

Library of Congress catalog card number: 2009939636
ISBN 978-0-06-156738-4

Typography by Rick Farley
10 11 12 13 LP/WOR 10 9 8 7
❖
First Edition

I Can Read!

READING
2
WITH HELP

DREAMWORKS

HOW TO TRAIN YOUR

DRAGON

Hiccup the Hero

Adapted by Catherine Hapka
Pencils by Charles Grosvenor
Color by Justin Gerard

HARPER
An Imprint of HarperCollinsPublishers

Hiccup did not fit in with
the other Vikings in his village.
Vikings were rough and tough.
Hiccup preferred to use his imagination
and invent things.

Every night,

dragons attacked the village.

Once, Hiccup hit one with

his new invention called the Mangler.

But no one believed Hiccup.

Not even his dad, Stoick.

The dragon attacks got worse.

It was time for the Viking teenagers

to go into training so they could

help defend the village.

At first Hiccup was happy.

Maybe now he could learn

to be a real Viking like his dad!

But on the first day of training,

he almost got blasted by a Gronkle.

Fighting dragons was tough work!

Hiccup felt terrible.

He went for a walk in the woods.

That's when he found something.

A dragon!

It was the dragon

Hiccup had hit with the Mangler.

Hiccup thought he was a goner.

But the dragon didn't try

to hurt him.

After that, Hiccup couldn't think
about anything else.
Why had the dragon let him live?
All Vikings knew that dragons
were nasty and dangerous.

Hiccup went back to see the dragon.

He brought it food

and named it Toothless.

Slowly, they became friends.

Hiccup soon figured out that his
new friend couldn't leave
the island as the other dragons did.
Toothless couldn't fly anymore.
Part of his tail was broken.

Hiccup wanted to help Toothless.

He invented a device

to fix the dragon's tail.

It took a few tries,

but finally Hiccup got it right.

Toothless could fly again,
as long as Hiccup helped steer.
They flew through the sky
together!

The other teenagers didn't know about
Hiccup's secret dragon friend.
All they knew
was that Hiccup was terrible
at dragon training.

Hiccup knew it, too.

He wanted to impress his dad,

but he couldn't fight even

the smallest dragon!

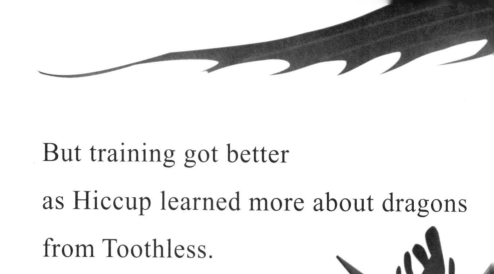

But training got better
as Hiccup learned more about dragons
from Toothless.

Hiccup learned that dragons love
dragon nip
and that they hate smoked eel.
Soon he was the best student
in the whole training ring.

Flying was getting better, too.
Together Hiccup and Toothless flew
every chance they got!
One day they flew all the way
to the dragons' island.

There, Hiccup saw
the dragons' terrible leader,
the Red Death.

Then something bad happened.

Stoick found out about Toothless!

He took the dragon prisoner.

Stoick wanted Toothless to show him
the way to Dragons Island
so he could wipe them out.
Hiccup was horrified.
He knew all dragons weren't evil.

Hiccup tried to explain
how strong the Red Death was,
and how he made the dragons
steal the Vikings' food.

But Stoick wouldn't listen.

The grownups left

to fight the dragons.

Hiccup knew the Vikings were doomed

unless he could save them.

Hiccup got the other teens to help.
He freed the training dragons
and showed his friends
how to fly them.

Soon the teens and dragons
were working as a team,
just like Hiccup and Toothless.
They all flew to Dragons Island.

29

The Vikings were losing the battle
against the giant Red Death.
Hiccup and his friends
joined the fight.

Everyone did their best.

But it was Hiccup and Toothless

who saved Stoick and the others.

They defeated the evil dragon leader!

Stoick gave Hiccup a proud hug.
Now Vikings and dragons
could be friends instead of enemies,
thanks to Hiccup the Hero!